The Animal Family

The Animal Family
by Randall Jarrell

DECORATIONS BY
Maurice Sendak

Alfred A. Knopf, New York

This is a Borzoi Book Published by Alfred A. Knopf, Inc.

Text copyright © 1965 by Random House, Inc. Illustrations copyright © 1965 by Maurice Sendak. All rights reserved under International and Pan-American Copyright Conventions. Published in the United States by Alfred A. Knopf, Inc., New York, and simultaneously in Canada by Random House of Canada Limited, Toronto. Distributed by Random House, Inc., New York. Originally published in hardcover by Pantheon Books, a division of Random House, Inc., New York, in 1965.
ISBN 0-394-88964-9 (pbk.)   ISBN 0-394-81043-0 (hardcover)
Library of Congress Catalog Card Number: 65-20659. Manufactured in the United States of America. First Knopf paperback edition   10   9   8   7   6   5   4   3

To Elfi
From Mary and Randall

Say what you like, but such things do happen—not often, but they do happen.

Contents

The Animal Family

THE HUNTER

Once upon a time, long, long ago, where the forest runs down to the ocean, a hunter lived all alone in a house made of logs he had chopped for himself and shingles he had split for himself. The house had one room, and at the end closest to the ocean there was a fireplace of pink and gray and green boulders—the hunter had carried them home in his arms from the cliff where the forest ended. On the crushed sea-shells of the floor there were deerskins and sealskins, and on the bed was the skin of a big black bear. Hanging on the wall over the bed were the hunter's bows and arrows.

The hunter, a big brown-faced man with fair hair and a fair beard, wore trousers and a shirt and shoes of creamy deerskin; his silvery gray cloak was made of the hide of a mountain lion; and the cap he wore when it rained or snowed was the skin of a sea-otter. Over the fireplace hung a big brass hunting horn he had found in a wreck the waves washed ashore. He had carved some of the logs of the walls and some of the planks of the chairs into foxes and seals, a lynx and a mountain lion. When he sat at night by the logs blazing in the

6

fireplace, the room looked half golden with firelight and half black with the shadow of the firelight, and the logs would roar and crackle so loudly that they drowned out the sound of the waves on the beach below.

But when the logs had burnt to embers and the embers had burnt away to coals, the man would lie in his bed, warm under the bearskin, and listen to the great soft sound the waves made over and over. It seemed to him that it was like his mother singing. And before he could remember that his father and mother were dead and that he lived there all alone, he had drifted off to sleep—and in his sleep his mother sat by the bed singing, and his father sat at the fireplace waxing his bowstring or mending his long white arrows.

In spring the meadow that ran down from the cliff to the beach was all foam-white and sea-blue with flowers; the hunter looked at it and it was beautiful. But when he came home there was no one to tell what he had seen—and if he picked the flowers and brought them home in his hands, there was no one to give them to. And when at evening, past the dark blue shape of a far-off island, the sun sank under the edge of the sea like a red world vanishing, the hunter saw it all, but there was no one to tell what he had seen.

8

One winter night, as he looked at the stars that, blazing coldly, made the belt and the sword of the hunter Orion, a great green meteor went slowly across the sky. The hunter's heart leaped, he cried: "Look, look!" But there was no one to look.

One evening he was lying on his bed. The soft summer breeze blew in through his open door, and the moonlight lay on the floor by the window like the skin of a white bear. The hunter thought; after a while his thoughts changed to dreams, and his mother was singing to him. But all at once his eyes were open, he was awake, and he could still hear someone singing. He got up and went down through the meadow to the sea. The tide was out. He walked over the warm wet sand, and the warm soft waves ran to his feet and died away whispering, in little foaming scallops like the scales of a fish.

Out at the seal rocks, hidden in their shadow, something was singing in a soft voice like a woman's. The song had words, but no words the hunter had ever heard before, and the song itself was different from any he had ever heard. He listened for a long time. The song ended on a long low note, and then everything was silent except the sea, whose shallow silver waves made a little hushing sound, and were silent for an instant, and then said *Hush!* again.

The hunter called to the singer. From the rocks' shadow he heard a quick scrambling noise, and then the sound of something diving into the water— the sound the seals always made. Shading his eyes with his hands, the hunter stared into the moonlight round the shadow of the rocks. But there was nothing to see and, now, nothing to hear. After a while he went home.

The next night when he heard the voice singing, and went down to the shore and listened till its new song was over, and then called softly to it, the singer dived into the water just as before; but this time, as the hunter stared

11

into the moonlight round the rocks, a sleek wet head came up out of the water, stared at him with shining eyes, and then sank back under and was gone. It was nothing he had ever seen before. Its long shining hair and shining skin were the same silvery blue-green, the color of the moonlight on the water. As he walked home over the sand of the beach and the grasses of the meadow, the hunter sang to himself, over and over, the last notes of the mermaid's song.

All the next day, no matter what he did, he hummed them; sometimes he would forget them for a few moments and be afraid he had forgotten them

12

for good, but they always came back to him. That night when the moon rose the hunter went down to the beach, sat at the edge of the water, and began to sing. He sang, one by one, all the songs he knew, and between each song and the next he would sing what he remembered of the mermaid's song. He kept looking toward the seal rocks: there was nothing. But after a while he saw, out past the first white line of the waves, a wet head.

Slowly, so as not to frighten her, he turned away; he went on singing. When he had almost finished the song he turned his head a little, and then a little more, till out of the corner of his eye

13

he could see that she had come closer—
the moonlight glistened on her hair and
on the wet curves of her shoulders.
Staring at her sidewise, he sang her her
own song. But when he was almost at
the end, he stopped in the middle of a
note. There was silence for a moment;
then he heard a little soft laugh, the
mermaid sang him the last notes of the
song, and before he could speak or
move she was gone—her head and
shoulders slid under the water so
smoothly that one minute she was there
and the next she had vanished without
a sound, almost without a ripple.

The hunter had lived so long with
animals that he himself was as patient

14

as an animal. He waited a long time, and then went home; he was not disappointed that she had gone, only certain that she would be back. He kept remembering how the laugh and the last notes of the song had sounded. When he was so nearly asleep that he could hardly tell whether he was remembering them or hearing them, he was still certain that she would be back—after he was fast asleep, neither thinking nor dreaming, he still smiled.

And the next night, and the next, and the next, and the next, she was there. She came closer, now; sitting in the shallow water, the waves not up to her waist, she talked to the hunter in a voice like the water. In a voice that made no more sense to the hunter than the water: no word of hers was like any word of his.

They began to teach each other words. The mermaid would touch her head and make the same sound over and over till the hunter had memorized it; then he would pat his leg and say "Leg! Leg!" and the mermaid, looking as if a leg were a very queer thing either to have or to have a word for, would repeat the word in her liquid voice.

But she could say his sounds so much better than he could say hers, remember his words so much better than he could remember hers, that before long the

16

learning was all one way. The hunter said her words awkwardly and ruefully, like something learned too late, but she said his like an old magician learning a new trick, a trick almost too easy for her to need to learn. The hunter said to her, bewildered: "You never make mistakes."

"What is mistakes?"

"The wrong word—the wrong sound, one you don't mean to make. The way I do. Mistakes are what *I* make when I try to talk the way you talk."

The mermaid repeated in a satisfied voice: "Mistakes." She had one more word.

She told the hunter that the others

like her used to come in as far as the
seal rocks, but had stopped now that he
was on the beach every night. She said:
"The sea—" then she stopped, at a loss
for the next word, and said: "You are
man. What is two? What is three?"

"Men."

"The sea men, like me—"

"The sea people."

"The sea peo-ple, like me, are afraid
of land. Not me. Oh, not me! They
think I—" here she hesitated, and then
said triumphantly—"make mistakes.
Make *bad* mistakes. They say, all good
comes from the sea." She struck the
water with a cheerful, scornful hand.

"Why don't you think that?"

18

The mermaid immediately told him, but in her language, not his. He laughed, she laughed and wrinkled her nose and forehead, searching for the words, but they wouldn't come, so she said, "Oh well!" Whenever she didn't know what to say or how to say it she would exclaim cheerfully, "Oh well!" The hunter couldn't remember ever teaching her to say it, but she had certainly learned.

But the next night she had her answer. Her first words were: "The land is new." The hunter gave her a puzzled look. She said swiftly, *"They* say all good comes from the sea. But the land is new. The land is—" here she said one of her own words, and then asked impatiently: "You have legs, I have not legs. The moon is white, the sky is black. What is that?"

"Different?"

"Different! Different! The land is *different*."

Sometimes the land was so different that the mermaid would learn a word in a few seconds and after a half-hour's explanation still not know what it meant. One day—the mermaid came to the beach in the daytime, now—the hunter pointed up over the meadow and said, in the clear divided tones of a teacher making something plain: "That is my *house*."

20

"House," hissed the mermaid. "House."

"I sleep in the *house,* on a *bed.* I eat in the *house,* on a *table.*"

"Bed," said the mermaid. "Table." But her quick eyes looked strained and hesitant; it was plain that she had no idea what the hunter was talking about.

The hunter started cheerfully, "A table's a big flat thing with legs"—the mermaid's eyes brightened: she knew what legs meant, and felt very landish for knowing—"that you eat on."

"Why do you get on it to eat?"

"Oh no, *you* don't get on it, you put what you're going to eat on it."

"Why?"

21

"Well, otherwise you'd have to hold it in your hands."

"You don't want to hold it in your hands?"

The hunter went on: "Then besides the table there's a bed. That's a big flat thing—"

"Oh yes, like a table."

"Well, not like a table exactly. It's made of wood like that log there, and has a bearskin on it, and you sleep in it."

The log was hollow; as she looked at it the mermaid saw. You took the log and put a skin around it, and then got inside it and went to sleep. "Ugh," said the mermaid. "I understand the bed."

22

"The bed and the table are both inside the house. The house is a big hollow thing—"

"Like the bed."

"No, the bed's not hollow."

"Then I don't understand the bed."

"We'll come back to the bed. The house is a big wooden thing—see how big it is—that you stay inside at night or when it rains."

"Why?"

"To keep from getting wet."

"To keep from getting *wet?*" the mermaid said despairingly.

All at once the hunter had an idea. "It's like a ship," he cried. "Wouldn't it be nice if, instead of just sleeping

anywhere, every night you swam inside
that wrecked ship by the reef and slept
there? And you could stay in it when
it rained."

The mermaid said softly, in utter
amazement: "That's the queerest thing
I've ever heard in all my life. You're—
you've made a mistake. You *must* have
made a mistake."

But usually whatever the hunter did
or said had for the mermaid the glamor
of land. She loved it when he shot for
her, and would run her hand along the
dark bow and white feathery arrows; as
she tugged at an arrow shot into driftwood from across the beach, she said
admiringly: "I think you could kill

24

anything." One day the hunter was sitting fishing; she swam up and said in a pleased, puzzled voice—she loved learning about things—"What are you doing?"

"Fishing."

The mermaid looked more puzzled than before, so the hunter explained in several sentences how he did it. She looked at him unbelievingly and then burst into laughter. "What are you laughing at?" asked the hunter.

"It's—it's such a *roundabout* way of catching fish."

"What do you want me to do—swim after them and catch them in my mouth?"

"You're the only thing I know that doesn't catch them that way! You look so helpless just sitting there waiting for one. Tell me what sort you want and I'll get it for you."

For a moment the hunter felt a child's humiliation. But then he laughed and told her the sort of fish he wanted, and the mermaid got it for him. The next day he brought her a piece of venison, which she took one bite of and threw away; but the day after he brought her a branch of red maple leaves. The mermaid looked at it as if she couldn't believe it; she carried it, and stroked it, and said to him lovingly, "It's the best thing I've ever had

26

in all my life. Oh, you're so lucky to live on land! The land's so—so—"

For the first time in many days she couldn't think of the word she wanted, and said as she had once said so often: "Oh well!"

By now the mermaid and the hunter were spending most of their time together. His house got to have a random half-lived-in look, and he hunted mechanically, for the next meal or two. The mermaid was used to the meadow, now; he and she would sit in the tan fall grass, looking out over the seal rocks to the island, and she would say triumphantly: "I am a hundred and fifty steps from the ocean. A hundred and fifty of your steps from the ocean!"

"Do you think any of the others have ever been so far up on the land?"

"Any of *them?* Oh no! If they saw me now they'd say"—she laughed and used her old word—" 'What a mistake you've made! Oh, what a mistake you've made!' "

Mistake or not, the mermaid had made it: that fall she went into the house with the table and the bed, and from then on the sea people saw her only as a visitor from the land that was "so—so—" whatever it was.

· II ·

THE MERMAID

After the mermaid had lived with the hunter for a while, he forgot that he had ever lived alone. The mermaid slept by him every night, but on top of the bearskin, not underneath it—she was used to the cold sea. And the bearskin on the bed, even the deerskins and seal-skins on the floor, weren't as smooth as the water she had always waked or slept in; she would run her hand over the softest fur, wrinkle up her nose, and say: "It's rough." But most of all she wanted the bed to rock; "it just stays still," she said disappointedly. The hunter made her a chair like a low heavy table, with two rockers underneath, and she would rock back and forth in it and stare at the fire.

She loved the fire. The first time she ever saw it she said, "Oh! Oh!" went over to it, and started to pick up one of the red coals. The hunter ran to her and pulled her away, but it was hard to make her understand; he had to put her hand close to the flames and let her almost burn herself, before she believed him. She put her fingers in her mouth, licked them, and then took them out and looked at them with a puzzled look. She said, "I didn't know there *was* anything

34

like that . . . Oh no, once there was! I touched an eel, a queer one, and it was like it."

She pointed to the coal, laughed, and said: "I thought it was a red shell, the best I ever saw. I was going to put it on the wall." Most of the plants under the sea are brown and green, and the bright things, there, are shells and fish; she would say, praising something, "It's like a shell." The first morning she looked out over the meadow and saw the spring flowers she cried, "Look, look! There're shells all over the meadow." She loved flowers and said that the birds, when they sang that first spring, sounded like flowers. "Gulls don't sing, they—bark," she told the hunter. He had told her one night that the noise the foxes made was barking.

"Once when I'd swum to the beach I heard a bird sing like that in the forest. But just once," she said. Now when she listened to the birds she would sing after them in a low voice, almost under her breath.

She loved the look of the fire, but she hated anything cooked over it—she ate nothing but raw fish, fish she herself had swum after and caught. (When one was particularly appetizing she couldn't resist offering the hunter a bite. "It's so good when you don't burn it in the fire," she would say.) She

36

helped the hunter with the cooking as a husband helps his wife: when he had gone out to hunt and had left something to stew, she would take the pot off the fire. But she never knew when to take it off; sometimes the meat was hard and sometimes it was cooked to pieces, and she never got it right except by accident. But when the accident happened the hunter would laugh and say, "You're as good a cook as my mother!" After all, why should he want her to keep house? If you had a seal that could talk, would you want it to sweep the floor?

The mermaid loved to bring the hunter shells, and starfish, and seahorses, and things from a wrecked ship at the bottom of the sea. Sometimes when she had brought him something new she would stare at everything old for an hour, and then rearrange half the things in the house. Once she brought the hunter something hidden in her hands, told him to shut his eyes, and then—getting it caught in his hair and beard—slipped it down over his head. "All right," she said, "now you can open your eyes."

When he opened them and looked down on his chest the hunter saw gold and green and blue stones, a necklace. He was so surprised that he almost said, "Men don't wear necklaces"; but instead he kissed the mermaid, turned the necklace around and around in his hands, and told her it was the best gift he had ever had. She said happily, "You can find anything down in the sea. The ships sail over us for a while but at last they sink—in the end everything comes to us."

The best thing she brought them was a ship's figurehead they put up over the door. It was all covered with barnacles and clams and mussels, but when they had scraped those off you could see the paint, even. It was a woman with bare breasts and fair hair, who clasped her hands behind her head; she wore a necklace of tiny blue flowers, and had a

garland of big flowers around her
thighs. But her legs and feet weren't a
woman's at all, but the furry, delicate,
sharp-hooved legs of a deer or goat—
and they were crossed at the ankles, as
if the bowsprit that she held up with
her head were no weight at all for her.
Her cheeks were rosy, as if the wind of
the ship's sailing had flushed them; and
her blue eyes stared out past you at
something far away.

. . . More even than she hated cooked
things, the mermaid hated anything
sweet. Once the hunter persuaded her
to try some berries: she sniffed uncer-
tainly at them, put them in her mouth,
and then spat them out, exclaiming:

40

"They're ugly, ugly! All gummy and blurry! How can you eat them?"

But honey was worst of all—she said, "It's like berries only it chokes you too. In all my life I've never tasted anything as bad." She drank salt water, always; when she tried the fresh water the hunter drank she said, "Water doesn't taste much, but your water doesn't taste any. It's hollow."

When she came from the sea to the house she would leave a trail of crushed grass and flowers through the meadow, and she would smell of them for a while; but she herself had a sharp salt smell, like the spray of a wave as it breaks across your face. Her blue eyes and her dark skin shone, and her teeth, when she smiled, were as white as foam.

At first she had thought the hunter's clothes part of him, and said in astonishment: "I thought you were brown and gray, but you're white. You're prettier when you're white." For a long time, whenever the hunter took off his clothes, she would laugh as if he were playing a trick on her, something magical but ridiculous. He would explain to her how useful and beautiful clothes are; she listened, always, with the same willing doubtful smile. She would have liked to be fooled, but it was more than she could manage; the hunter was the one clothed thing in a naked world.

42

No matter how cold it was, she never wore any clothes herself; sometimes she would take a red fox-fur and tie it around her wrist for a bracelet. And because once, out on the seal rocks, she had put a wreath of seaweed on her head, the hunter carved her one out of myrtle wood, with leaves and berries almost like the real ones; she wore it at dinner sometimes.

When it rained the hunter stayed inside. He would carve something, or sharpen his axe, or make himself arrows, or do housework, or play games with the mermaid, to keep himself from being bored. The mermaid couldn't understand why he wanted to be inside when it rained; to her it made no difference. One day when he came in after being caught in a hard rain, she said to him, touching the sodden leather of his shirt: "It's because you wear clothes. The rain gets them all cold and heavy. If you didn't wear clothes you wouldn't mind the rain." Nor could she understand why he got bored—she never understood, even, what it meant to be bored. She said, "If you're tired of doing something, why, you can do something else. But why do you have to do something?"

She would lie curled up in the window-seat—they had a big window of glass and wood from a ship, and a win-

44

dow-seat by it, all full of furs—and would look out to sea, or doze, or just be. She never seemed to feel that she needed to say anything; she would sit silent for hours and then answer him, when he said something, with as much animation as if she had been talking all the time. Sometimes her saying nothing, doing nothing, troubled the hunter. "What are you thinking?" he would ask. Now and then the mermaid told him, but usually she would answer with her old "Oh well!" and the little indifferent wrinkling of the nose that, with her, was the equivalent of a shrug.

The hunter and the mermaid played checkers and jackstraws and a game like horseshoes, throwing rings over a stake. But they quit the ring-game because the mermaid missed so seldom. When, once in twenty or thirty times, the ring would bounce off the stake, she would laugh and say perplexedly, "I did it wrong! I don't understand it, I did it wrong."

But whenever *anything* went wrong she laughed and thought it funny; once, shifting the horn and the shells over the mantle, she fell and dented the horn, broke two shells, and knocked the breath out of herself—and as soon as she got her breath back she began to laugh. It was almost the only time the hunter had seen her lose her breath: she could hold her breath for half an hour, like a whale or dolphin. She would do it to amuse him, occasionally pointing to her closed mouth and narrowed nostrils. And she could balance herself on anything, juggle with anything, like a seal.

She learned the hunter's language so well that at last she thought in it. (Except when she was in the water: "When the water touches me I think the way I always thought," she said.) She taught the hunter a little more of her own langauge, but it was hard for him to say. When she spoke it, it was like water gurgling in a cleft in the rock. But whatever she said sounded like that: she had learned the hunter's words, but she said them to the sea's tune.

She taught the hunter to say in Dolphin and Seal, in case he were ever swept to sea: "Help me! Help me to the beach!" Learning that sentence in Dolphin was the hardest thing the hunter had ever done. He told her indignantly: "You have to say it with the roof of your mouth and your nose, and so high you can't even hear yourself say it."

"That's right, that's right!" said the mermaid. "Now you're getting it."

She liked Dolphin and looked down on Seal. "Dolphins say as much as the people say," she told the hunter, "but most of the words in Dolphin are too

48

high for us, we can't say them. But seals don't say much—Seal is easy. You can learn all the Seal there is in a week."

The hunter would tell her about his father and mother and the years the three of them had lived there. (There was a thin square piece of lace left from those years, the mother's handkerchief; to the hunter and the mermaid it was a great treasure. "How did they ever make all those little holes in it?" she asked the hunter; but he didn't know.) The mermaid tried to imagine what their life had been like, but it was hard for her. "You're the only man I've ever seen," she sad. "Except drowned ones." So he carved for her, out of walnut, a statue of his father and a statue of his mother. When she saw his mother's long skirts she said, "Why, she's like me!" But when she saw the carving of his father she laughed and laughed. "You didn't have to do that one," she said. The hunter didn't know what she meant or why she laughed, and looked at her uneasily and disappointed, so that she kissed him and said, "It's just like you! There's no difference at all, it's just like you!"

She would tell him the sea people's stories, and he would tell her the fairy tales his mother had told him; when he said nursery rhymes to her, she would laugh as if she were being tickled. (She

50

loved to be tickled.) "I like it when it sounds the same," she said. "Show me how to make it sound the same myself."

After a while she knew all the nursery rhymes by heart. Sometimes on a stormy day, working away at something, the hunter would look up to hear what she had said, and she would be lying there looking out at the waves, saying softly:

> "Hickory dickory dock,
> The mouse ran up the clock."

... Whenever anything reminded the hunter of his father and mother, you could see that he missed them and longed to have them alive again. The mermaid would tell him about her child-hood and her family and her sister, the dead one, but she never seemed to want any of it back. The hunter said, puzzled: "Don't you wish your sister were still here?"

The mermaid answered: "She was then. Why do you want her to be now too?" The hunter remembered that he had never seen the mermaid cry; he thought with a little shiver, "Do mermaids cry?"

The only things the mermaid was afraid of were big sharks and killer whales. "They kill us if they catch us," she told him. But she was afraid of them in a matter-of-fact, indifferent

52

way, and said that none of her people really thought about them or hated them. "Why should we?" she said. "They eat us the way we eat fish. The fish don't hate us. They swim next to us when they know we're not hungry, and when we're hungry they get away from us if they can. Everything lives on everything."

At first she would say, "I'll go home," when she went back to visit her family. But after a while she called the house with the hunter home. The first day she was back from the sea she would lie in the window-seat and shift back and forth and shake her head with a puzzled look. She told the hunter: "In the sea everything moves, and when I come back to where it's all still it makes me dizzy, everything seems to roll back and forth. I can't get it to stay still."

In a little she laughed and said, "When I tell them about home they don't believe it. They don't believe we have a fire—I tell them, but they don't believe in fire. I show them how it lights our window at night, but they think it's like the waves in summer, when they shine, or like a star."

The hunter and the mermaid were so different from each other that it seemed to them, finally, that they were exactly alike; and they lived together and were happy.

54

· III ·

THE HUNTER BRINGS HOME A BABY

But after the hunter and the mermaid had lived together a long time, the hunter began to have a dream. He would say in the morning to the mermaid, with a troubled look: "I had my dream."

"I'm sorry," she would answer.

"It was the same as ever," the hunter went on, looking out into the air as though the dream were still there for him to see. "My father was standing by the fire and he was double, like a man and his shadow—I was his shadow.

And my mother sat there singing, and she was double too, like a woman and her shadow; and when I looked at it you were her shadow. But when I looked over to where I used to lie on the floor by the fire, there was nothing, not even a shadow; the place was empty. And the empty place got dark, and the fire went out, and I woke."

"It's a bad dream," the mermaid said, frowning.

The hunter said, "I hope I never dream it again." Every few weeks, though, he would dream it. Finally the mermaid said to him: "I know what your dream means. It means you want a boy to live with us. Then you'll be your

60

father's shadow, and I'll be your mother's, and the boy will be yourself the way you used to be—it will all be the way it used to be."

The hunter thought for a moment. Then he nodded; he could see that what she said was so. But there was nothing he could do about it: they had no child themselves, and out in the wilderness there were no human beings from whom they could beg or borrow or steal a child.

One day the man was hunting. The night came and he hadn't come home—it got later and later, darker and darker, and he still hadn't come. The mermaid would go outside and look up toward the forest and the mountains, but she could see nothing. It began to rain. The big drops beat on the roof and against the window, and the wind roared in the trees outside; but finally the rain and clouds blew out to sea, the stars came out, and the wet black night was silent except for the sound of the waves. The mermaid lay in the window-seat half awake and half asleep . . . All at once there were footsteps, the door opened, and the hunter staggered in with something in his arms. He said to the mermaid, laughing: "I've a boy for us."

"What's happened to you! What's happened to you!" the mermaid cried.

There were three long cuts down the side of the hunter's face, and the blood had dripped from them onto his wet, naked shoulder; there were terrible bruises all along his back and chest; and he held in his arms, smothered inside his wet deerskin shirt, something that struggled to get free, and snapped up at the man's face, and made a queer angry miserable sound, half a whine and half a growl. The mermaid looked at its brown furry head and its big teeth and shining eyes, and saw that it was a bear cub.

"If I hadn't had an arrow out I'd never have got home to you," the hunter answered. "It was getting dark and I was going through some bushes full of berries when I heard that sound a bear makes to her cubs, and before I could take two steps she was on me—I'd come between her and *him*.

"I shot her from so close the arrow went half through her. She was so near I couldn't run, I couldn't dodge, even; her claws came here—" he touched the side of his face—"she hugged me to her so hard I thought my back would break, and then I drove my knife in her from behind. I had my left arm in front of my face, and I could feel her teeth going into it through the leather. She shook me the way a grown-up shakes a child, I thought, 'I'm done for,' and

64

then she went limp all over and fell down on top of me and never moved again. And for a while I couldn't move myself, I just lay there. Look where her teeth went in my arm." He held out his left arm—the right was still hugging the cub in the shirt—and halfway between the wrist and the elbow she could see the regular, bloody pattern of the bear's teeth.

The hunter plopped the bundle of wet leather and bear cub down onto the bearskin of the bed; and while the mermaid washed the hunter's face and arm and shoulder, the cub struggled out of the shirt, crawled back into the farthest corner of the bed, and growled and growled at them. "He was in a tree," the hunter said. "If he'd been a month older I could never have got him down. Oh, he was hard to get home! He snapped and wriggled the whole way."

When the hunter was dressed and dry they had their dinner. It felt like a holiday to them, somehow; they laughed as they ate. As he smelled the food the cub came out to the center of the bear-skin, and the hunter threw him a piece of meat. The little bear growled and backed away, but then sidled up to the meat, hit it with his paw, and began to shake it. When he had gulped it down the mermaid threw him another piece, and another; finally she held some out

66

in her hand, and he came to the edge of the bed and reached for it. The hunter said with a peaceful smile: "In a couple of days he'll be eating at the table."

That night they put deerskins and sealskins on the bed and let the cub sleep on the bearskin, in the corner. Sometimes he would wake and cry for a while, and then huddle in the corner with his face pushed into the bearskin, and go back to sleep. And in two days he was sitting on the floor by the table when they ate, eating with them; in a week it was as if he had lived with them always.

·IV·
THE BEAR

The bear's wet nose was cold and shiny, and he stuck it into everything. He had beautiful fur—it was denser and shinier than the bearskin on the bed, even—and it wasn't black but a soft deep brown. The palms of his paws were as pink as a man's palms, but fringed with five little gray-blue, steely claws; he had one special log that he liked to sharpen them on. The mermaid would feel them and marvel that their pet had such hard sharp claws; and the hunter seemed gentle to her, too, so that

71

she said to him once, feeling the razory heads on his arrows, "It's queer for *you* to have things like that."

The hunter said with a smile that bared his white teeth: "We've all got them, I guess."

"That's right," admitted the mermaid, baring hers.

The bear loved for the hunter and the mermaid to pet him or push him or hit him or roll him over—his motto seemed to be, "Go ahead, it won't hurt *me*." He would sit up and they would toss the leather ball to him in a gentle arc, and he would catch it in his mouth or bat at it with his paws, scrambling after it when he missed it. He sat up and begged very beautifully, and he could walk on two legs almost as well as on four; when he would walk across the room on his hind legs, reach for something on the table, and then cram it into his mouth, he looked like a little boy in a bearskin.

But not for long. He grew so fast that they couldn't believe it; by the time the geese flew south that fall the hunter could barely lift him. It was no wonder that he grew so: everything they gave him, everything that he came across in the meadow or in the forest or on the beach, he ate. The mermaid said, "Why, if you put his chair in his bowl, he'd eat it." Wood-rats and meadow-

mice, meadow-grass, buttercups, roots
and nuts and seeds and buds, grubs,
worms, insects, blackberries and blue-
berries and raspberries and wild grapes,
clams and mussels and crabs, honey and
honeybees, any sort of fish they fed him,
any sort of meat they fed him—he
gulped it all down.

They set a place for him at dinner, a
bowl and a little low chair like the mermaid's, but without any rockers. (At
first they had put his bowl of water on
the table, but he always knocked it over,
so after that they left it in the corner.)
The bear's table manners were bad. But
so were the mermaid's—especially as
she couldn't resist throwing the bear

pieces of fish. Catching them was what the bear did best: his muzzle would dart out and his teeth ring shut on them with magical swiftness and certainty, so that you never would have believed how badly he ate out of his bowl.

But really all of them ate as they pleased; the hunter would cut off big pieces of meat with his knife, chew away at them and gulp them down, all the while talking eagerly—he had long ago forgotten how his father and mother ate and made him eat.

The bear had no napkin, of course, but neither did the hunter and the mermaid; they wiped their mouths on their arms. At least, though, they didn't lick themselves. The bear licked himself with such big bobbing strokes of his head that he almost lost his balance and fell off his chair.

One night the mermaid watched him for a while and said: "He certainly is an inexperienced washer. The more he washes himself the worse he gets."

"The more he washes himself the worse he looks," said the hunter. "All he does is to get himself wet and rumpled and make his fur stick out every which way. Well, at least he never washes long."

"He never does anything long except eat and sleep," the mermaid replied.

This was so. After he had just eaten,

76

the bear had a particularly satisfied, good-humored look: his little eyes would twinkle at them, and he would look round benignantly. But soon his wandering eyes would glaze, his eyelids would steal shut, and snap open, and then steal shut again, and he would be fast asleep.

"We are two," the mermaid would say to the hunter.

"You certainly don't have to think of anything for *him* to do after dinner. Not old Eat-and-Sleep," the hunter said.

The bear began to snore. The mermaid said, "You—*walrus!*"

They couldn't help making fun of

their bear. It felt good, somehow. He sat there like a hill having a nap after dinner, and the mermaid said, yawning: "Having him's very soothing—you get the feeling that nothing can happen to him *or* you."

The bear rolled out of his chair; he took two staggering steps toward the fireplace, fell down, and was fast asleep again.

"Old Eat-and-Sleep!" said the hunter contentedly.

. . . The bear was a remarkable tree-climber: he hung on to the trunk with his front feet and kicked himself up with his hind feet, his paws churning and his claws making big gouges in the

78

trunk. Like some animal that doesn't know how to climb a tree, never has known how to climb a tree, but thinks it will just try anyway, the bear went up the trunk by main force; and he didn't so much climb down as fall, interrupting his plunge with five or six desperate momentary pauses. If it was an autumn day on which he was climbing, he would end surrounded by nuts and branches and, grunting contentedly, would start to gobble up the nuts.

One cold afternoon in late autumn, when the hunter came home from the forest, the mermaid met him at the door.

"Come quick, come quick!" she said,

seizing him by the arm. Her face was worried and miserable—the hunter had never seen her look so miserable.

"What is it?" the hunter said.

"He's dying," the mermaid said. "I reached in and touched him and he didn't move, he didn't even know I was there. And he's barely breathing—he takes a little faint slow breath and then doesn't breathe at all, you can count six or seven before he takes another breath."

"Oh, Lord!" said the hunter. "I knew I should have looked for him when he didn't come home last night. Where is he?"

"Up at the cliff. In the tall cave—

the narrow one, the one you can barely get inside."

They hurried off. "Maybe it was another bear and he crawled there because he was hurt so bad he couldn't get home," the hunter called back over his shoulder. "Was he bleeding much?"

"No, not a bit," the mermaid answered. "He's—"

But the hunter, running as fast as he could go, was already too far off to hear her. The mermaid toiled along up the path; when she got near enough to the cliff to see the cave, the hunter had disappeared. She went to the mouth of the cave and peered inside. The hunter was bending over the bear, feeling him, and the bear didn't move.

All at once the hunter straightened up, took a step toward her, and started to laugh. Hearing his echoing laugh, down there in the darkness of the cave, was frightening to the mermaid; but he had such a relieved sound that she cried, "He isn't dying? He's all right?"

"He's never been better off in his life," said the hunter. "I forgot you didn't know. He's just asleep—asleep for the winter."

"For the *winter?*"

"Bears sleep all winter. You know how fat he's been getting—well, he'll lie here fast asleep till spring, unless there's a warm spell."

"And it's all right for him to breathe like that?"

"That's the way they all do. You can't wake them. Watch!" He got hold of the bear below the shoulders, pulled him up as far as he could, and began to shake him. He shook and shook, and then gave a tremendous shout, one that made the mermaid's ears ring.

Not even the bear's breathing changed.

"How *queer!*" said the mermaid. "How *queer!* Oh, I'm so glad he's all right."

The hunter lowered the bear to the ground, patted him affectionately, and then climbed out of the cave. The mer-

maid said, "I think I'll pat him too."
She did, and then said sorrowfully,
"He won't be with us all winter? Every
winter?"

The hunter remembered something
the mermaid had said about her sister,
and said, laughing: "He was all summer. Why do you want him all winter
too?"

"Oh, I don't know. I'm—I'm used
to him."

They often talked about him, that
winter; occasionally the hunter would
go out to the cave and come back with a
cheerful, "Fast asleep!" Once the mermaid answered, "It's like that story of
your mother's."

84

"Like what?"

"Like that story. You know, the Sleeping Beauty one. It's like having that Sleeping Beauty for a pet."

They did miss him; and when at last, one foggy morning in March, there was a scratching at the door, and a thin, grumpy, famished bear stuck his nose in over the threshold, they fed him thankfully. How he ate! And how he grew! By the end of the summer he was so big that, when he ran, he looked like a bed galloping across the meadow: you could hardly believe that so big a thing could move so fast.

The bigger the bear got, the wetter the bear got; and there is nothing so noticeable as a wet bear. It rained on the bear, the bear forded streams, the bear fished—he would sit or stand in the little river that came down to the sea, with the water boiling up over his back, and snap or bat at the fish swimming up through the white water. And, finally, when the rain was over, the river crossed, the fish eaten, the bear would come home.

The first year it was like having a wet St. Bernard come home; the second year he was more like a wet Shetland pony; the third year he was like a wet horse in a wet overcoat. Drying him was like drying a marsh: they could have taken everything in the house, rubbed him with it, and in the end they and everything in the house would have been wet and the bear still not dry.

He would sit by the fireside in a little pool of water, his fur would steam and the pool of water would steam, steam would cover the glass of the window, he would start to shake himself—

"No, no! No, no!" the hunter and the mermaid would shout. And the bear, their trained bear, *wouldn't* shake himself: he had learned that when they shouted "No, no!" it meant he mustn't shake himself. Outside, of course, he did. The hunter had once measured, on the beach, the circle the bear made when he shook himself; from the wet center to the imprint of the last scattered drops was seventeen steps.

. . . The bear's life was placid and uneventful, and he snored or shuffled or galloped through it, grunting in satisfaction; occasionally, though, he met with accident. One warm soft afternoon the hunter and the mermaid were sitting inside talking when the bear burst through the doorway, bounded to the bed and, thrashing and plunging, tried to dig himself in under the bearskin. Just behind him was a cloud of—"Bees! Bees!" cried the hunter, slapping his neck.

"Bees?" said the mermaid. Then she gave a shriek and clutched her shoulder

88

—another bee had landed. The hunter seized her, heaved her up into his arms, and staggered out the door. As he ran he heard the bear groan: some of the bees must have got in under the bear-skin. There were dozens of them just behind the hunter and the mermaid—"*Oh!*" screamed the mermaid, as one of them caught up.

The hunter ran, very awkwardly and very fast, across the meadow to the beach. The tide was in. He splashed through the shallow water, gave two desperate plunges that carried them out waist-deep, and then fell headlong; the mermaid, flying out of his arms, disappeared into the next wave.

Almost before they could get their heads out of the water the bees were on them. Snorting and blowing, his eyes and nose full of sea-water, the hunter heaved and plunged and splashed—a perfect fountain of water and spray rose over him. The mermaid imitated him faithfully for a moment, then lost her balance, fell over, and began to splash as hard as she could with her tail.

For the bees it was like trying to get at two geysers undersea: wet, cold and discouraged, they began to make larger and larger circles around the two, and a few of them even turned back toward the beach. "We're getting them! Splash! Splash!" shouted the hunter. In five minutes the last bee was flying sulkily over the beach toward the meadow, the hunter was sitting there panting, with the water up to his neck, and the mermaid was laughing—she laughed so hard that she strangled, stopped till she could get her breath, and then started to laugh all over again. The hunter began to laugh himself.

"We're getting them! Splash! Splash!" cried the mermaid, pointing at the hunter and laughing harder than ever.

"If that's the way you take it," said the hunter, "I won't give you any advice next time."

The mermaid answered, "Just so long

as you carry me. How'd you ever get us here so fast?"

The hunter said, "I must have been inspired. Oh, that bear of ours! Either we've got to train him to leave bee-trees alone or else we've got to keep the door shut."

"Let's teach him to run for the beach instead of his bearskin. We can tell him, 'You're a big bear now.' "

"I'll go see how it is up at the house," the hunter said. He was soon back. "There're dozens still flying in and out of the door. I don't know where *he* is— you can see they're just doing it out of habit. They'll be gone by sunset."

That night as the two of them were

92

sitting by the fire, all serene except for the clay they'd put on their stings, something scratched at the door. The hunter opened it and the bear came in. Evidently he had ended in the water himself: he was sodden. But the water hadn't washed away the big gummy smears of honey and beeswax on his head and shoulders—there were dead bees caught in his fur, even. He sat down and began to lick his right front paw; the bare palm had several swollen places on it where the bees had stung him. "Just look at his poor nose!" said the mermaid. It was so swollen that, like a man with the mumps, the bear didn't even resemble himself.

And yet he didn't look dissatisfied or miserable, but just sat by them licking his fur, as if he were home and glad to be home. The harder he licked the more of a mess he made of himself. As the fire got his wet fur warmer and warmer, a little cloud of steam rose from him; he smelled like four or five wet dogs and a beehive.

Before long his contented, shining eyes began to get a blurred look. "He's had a full day," the hunter said.

"If he's got as much honey inside as outside, he's a full bear," the mermaid replied.

"*And* wax—*and* bees. Remember, bears eat bees too."

94

"Is there anything anybody in the whole world eats that they don't eat? Have we ever found a single thing that he won't eat?"

"Oh, wood."

"If it's dead wood he turns it over and rips it up and eats all the grubs and bugs inside. And if it's a live tree he bats at the branches till he's got all the nuts off and then he eats them. And if it's spring he eats the buds and the blossoms and the bark on the—"

"You're right," the hunter said.

The bear's eyes had closed; he began to snore. It was a gentle, peaceable sound. He looked as if he had spent the day dozing by the fireside.

"He's got a real gift for getting along in the world," the hunter said admiringly. "Doesn't he look *innocent?*"

The mermaid said: "To think we used to live without a bear!"

·V·
THE LYNX

One day in early spring the mermaid came back from the sea: she had spent three days with her own people. The hunter must have been watching for her—he met her in the meadow. When they got to the door of the house he said to her, trying to keep from smiling: "I've got a surprise for you."

"The bear's back!"

"No, he's still in the cave. But you're warm. When you get inside, tell me if you see anything different." The mermaid went in and looked eagerly, then carefully, around. There were flames in the fireplace, and shells and the hunting horn over the fireplace; the bearskin was on the bed, the deerskins and sealskins were on the floor, the bows and arrows were on the wall—

"It must be a small surprise," the mermaid said.

"A big one for his age," the hunter answered matter-of-factly. "Look in the bottom drawer."

The bottom drawer of the chest by the bed was open, so that you could see inside it the silver and white, deerskin confusion of the hunter's shirts. "I'll straighten your shirts," the mermaid

102

said automatically; with the years she had become a spasmodic, enthusiastic housekeeper who straightened the room at the same speed at which she caught salmon.

"Oh, do!" said the hunter, laughing disproportionately. But when the mermaid reached down to the drawer, the drawer hissed at her. She sprang back. There in the middle of the drawer, white, silver, and gray as the shirts, was a spotted kitten as big as a cat; his tremendous silver eyes met the mermaid's and, shrinking into the corner, he gave a hiss that would have done credit to a sea-serpent.

"Another boy," said the hunter

equably. "I got lonesome without you *or* the bear."

"No, what's it really?"

"A lynx. A baby lynx."

"How on earth did you get it?"

"I stole him. The mother has four more, and she'll never miss him—I don't think she can count up to five, anyway."

"But how did you get it without her knowing?"

"She lives in a cave up in the hills. I saw her feeding them outside it. I was downwind from them, and none of them smelled me. You should have seen them playing with what she'd feed them; it was the way the bear used to be

104

when he was little, only more so. A lot more so.

"After that I'd go by every once in a while—believe me, I was careful—and I'd see them playing on the rocks outside the cave. Their mother wanted them to stay inside, I guess, but they didn't want to. This one's the bravest of the bunch; when I went by the day you left he was forty feet from the mouth of the cave. I thought, 'Somebody's going to snap *you* up.' And I was right, somebody did."

"But how long will it take to tame him?"

"He's tame now where I'm concerned—he just doesn't know you yet.

Watch!" The mermaid went over to her chair, sat down, and watched. The hunter held out his hand to the kitten in a way that was neither fast nor slow, careless nor careful, but that seemed to take it for granted that the little lynx wanted the hunter to touch him; and the lynx didn't hiss, didn't shrink back, but let the hunter scratch him under the chin— in a moment he was purring.

"Why does he make that gratey noise?" the mermaid asked. She had never heard a cat purr; for that matter, she had never seen a cat except once, and it had been a bobcat fifty yards off in the forest.

"That's purring," the hunter said.

106

"Cats do it when they feel good. And look, he's kneading his paws!" The lynx's purr had got louder and louder, and he was working his claws in and out of the shirts, with a look of absent, ecstatic satisfaction on his face.

"Why do you call it kneading his paws?"

"I don't know, that's what my mother called it. The cat on the boat did it. I don't know what it means."

"Kneading his paws," repeated the mermaid, and put the phrase by *purring;* for the first time in many months she had some new words.

"He's *very* playful," said the hunter proudly. "He plays as much in a day as

107

the bear played in a week. You ought to
see him with a ball!" He went over, got
the ball, and rolled it past the drawer;
the lynx was on it in one bound. He gave
the ball two immense, instantaneous
bites, batted it from one paw to the
other, flung it into the air, and then
began to chase it around the room. He
was doing it all himself, but you could
never have told that from looking at
him or from looking at the ball—the
ball came to life and the lynx was
after it. When the ball stopped he
would hide behind some inch-high fold
in a deerskin and then with agonizing
slowness, as carefully as a man walking
a wire over an abyss, would work his

108

invisible way up to the ball.

"He makes a sort of story out of it," said the mermaid, enchanted. The lynx sprang. "He's too clever for it. Poor ball, it hasn't a chance!"

"Look how big his paws are!" the hunter said. "And they'll always look that big, even when he's grown up— that's how they can walk on snow so well. And see how long his hind legs are!"

"Why, they're ever so much longer than his front legs," the mermaid said surprisedly. "Is that why he can jump so high?" The hunter had just tossed the ball to the lynx in a slow careful arc, and the lynx had met it in mid-air.

"Oh, he can jump higher than *that!* He can jump to the top of the chest already. I'll bet you that in a month he'll be jumping all the way to the rafters."

The hunter would have lost his bet, but only by a week. After that the rafters were a kind of special tree-top kingdom all the lynx's own. Usually he jumped from the floor to the top of the chest, and then jumped to the rafters; but if he had to, he could tense himself all over, make a couple of false starts, and then shoot up to a rafter in one soaring, unbelievable bound. It was dark up there; the lynx went comfortably from rafter to rafter, and then lay with his big serious head—after the first month or two he stopped looking like a kitten—stretched flat on his out-stretched paws, watched, thought, dozed. The bigger he got, the stranger it was to see him in the rafters: set there in the air above their heads like a cloud by moonlight, staring at them with his big steady silver eyes, he looked mag-ical, a spell the forest had cast on the house.

From the first the lynx loved being with the bear; he had started out with one big furry thing, his mother, and the bear was bigger and furrier. When he stretched himself against that great brown mound, so awkward and oblivious, the lynx looked very quick and smooth and small. Away from the bear, he looked quick and smooth and big. How deftly he sat at the table, delicately eating and drinking from his dish and bowl, purringly taking a bit of fish from the mermaid's fingers! (They had given him the bear's chair—the bear had long ago outgrown it, and sat on the floor by the table now, his head and shoulders towering above it.) The lynx had the best table manners of them all, except when they served him partridge: he loved it so much that he would dab at his piece with his paw, work it out of his dish onto the table, and then with a rapt stare rub his head against it—once

112

he got so excited that he flung it into the air, batted it to the floor, and then chased it around the room as if it were his ball.

The bear's growing up had been one long accident; the lynx grew up as smoothly and designedly as he did everything else. The first time he got on the roof, even, he managed to get down by himself, after the mermaid and the hunter had told him and told him and told him he could. But one day the hunter left the top drawer of the chest open, the one that held his mother's handkerchief; when they came back the rumpled deerskins were in piles on the floor, and the lynx, still looking slightly out of breath, was lying in the corner with the wet, shredded handkerchief a few inches from his nose.

"Oh, what a *shame!*" said the mermaid.

"It's not his fault," the hunter said sadly. "He doesn't know any better." He reached down and patted the lynx and the lynx purred. But after they'd washed and dried the handkerchief and put it back in the drawer, it was as good as ever, in its way; and it had become a sort of lynx-souvenir too, a reminder of the only real mistake their lynx had ever made.

. . . The lynx not only hunted for

himself, he hunted for the family; it was his idea, not the family's. He brought them, mostly, rabbits. At first the hunter and the mermaid were full of encouragement: after all, it *was* wonderful that so young a lynx could catch so many rabbits. But the morning the mermaid woke at dawn and found three rabbits, slightly bloody, in a pile at the bottom of the bed, with the proud lynx asleep beside them, she said to the hunter: "We're getting to be a perfect rabbit-warren. Three already, and it's still not light out!"

"Tell him no, no!" said the hunter drowsily.

"He's asleep."

"So am I," the hunter answered, turning over.

But after a few days of their saying firmly, "It's *your* rabbit," and then carrying it outside, the lynx padding misunderstandingly along, he got to see that they were indifferent—hostile even —to rabbits. They were no better about squirrels and seemed shocked, almost, when he brought them a fox. But the hunter was grateful for the partridge the lynx would bring. "They're good and a lot of trouble to hunt," he said. "I hate carrying along blunt arrows. If you can bear waking up and finding them on the foot of the bed—"

"Oh, I don't mind," the mermaid

116

answered. "Just as long as it's not honey."

The bear had never been an ideal walking-companion: it was like taking along a bed or a table that kept turning over logs for grubs. But the lynx was quieter and quicker and noticed more than you yourself did—he had a big cat's curiosity about the world. In the forest he investigated the lower branches as easily and noiselessly as the ground; when they got to tall grass he would cross it in a few easy, tremendous bounds, soaring up over everything like a great silver grasshopper; and he went up and down the beach as if he had been raised on one, padding along on

117

the wet sand at the edge of the surf, sniffing at driftwood and seaweed and occasionally rushing at some just-wary-enough sea-bird that would shoot up with a squawk.

Sometimes the lynx would bound up, fresh from finding something a hundred yards away, and would try hard to lead them to it, rubbing against the hunter's legs and purring, and then starting off with an enticing little rush. His notions of what the two of them would find interesting were rather lynxish notions, often ending in an "Oh, is *that* all!" from the mermaid or the hunter; but his notions of what would interest a bear were a bear's—the bear gobbled it

118

up. The lynx loved to give you something or to get you to go somewhere: he did both with a pleased, eager, bewitching look, as if it were wonderful for him, wonderful for you, wonderful, wonderful!

The bear was fond of the hunter and the mermaid, but the lynx adored them; as they said, "All you have to do is start to touch him and he purrs." Mostly he had a bass purr, like distant thunder, but when he felt particularly ecstatic his purr got a queer high throaty sound, like a basso singing falsetto. He sat by the two of them, and rubbed against them, and followed them around, and stared at them with an absorbed satisfied stare; in the morning when they woke up he was so glad to see them again that he would give them little affectionate mock-bites—it was almost like tickling, and would make the mermaid laugh and laugh. "Ouch!" the hunter would say. "Easy! easy!" It worked, too; for a moment the lynx's teeth would barely touch him.

What tickled the mermaid even more was for the lynx to finish washing himself and to start out on the two of them. He would go to work on the hunter's hair or beard and give it a long, sober, absorbed licking, till it looked all wet and shining; meanwhile the hunter lay back on the bed in drowsy acquiescence

120

and the mermaid made little speeches of admiration: "If I hadn't lived with you so long I don't know whether I'd recognize you. He's got you so you just gleam!"

"In a minute you'll be gleaming yourself," the hunter said; and before long the lynx was hard at work on the mermaid. This wasn't so quiet a job, though, since the mermaid kept laughing a string of little bubbling glistening laughs as the tiny barbs of the lynx's tongue tickled her. Oddly, the lynx never tried to wash the bear; he must have seen that though the bear was foolish enough to try it, washing the bear was too much even for the bear.

When all this was over the lynx
would lie beside them, one paw out-
stretched, like a lion on a monument.
It was remarkable how serious and
beautiful his big face always looked.
Most of the dusky spots and dark
bands that had marked him a kitten
had disappeared or were fainter now. In
winter he was a long-furred, full-bodied,
gray-and-white animal, but in summer
he was thin and gray and brown, almost
lanky, though his thoughtful silver-
eyed face stayed as impressive as ever.
Two astonishingly long black-and-silver
tufts of fur jetted from the tips of his
gray ears; there were little vertical gray-
black stripes in the center of his fore-

122

head, as though he were thinking seriously about something; and the big
snowdrifts of fur that covered his
cheeks and jaws and neck were striped
with three beautiful black bars, the biggest of them running all the way up to
the outer corners of his eyes. His big
clear eyes were outlined in delicate
black, with four or five fine dark mark-
ings above each; each of the bristling
antenna-like hairs that sprang from his
white muzzle was matched by a tiny
black dot; and his little bobbed-off
fawn-and-silver tail was jet-black at the
tip. In the winter the lynx's fur was so
long and fine and beautiful that you
couldn't look at it without wanting to

touch him—all summer, though, his fur had a sketchy, temporary feel, as though he had taken off his real coat for the hot weather and were wearing a rough substitute.

After his third year with them, the lynx didn't grow any larger, but as the mermaid said, he didn't need to: he was *big*. "Even when he plays," she went on, "he's so serious and—and—what did you tell me the king was in the story?"

The hunter thought for a moment and said: "Noble."

"That's right," said the mermaid, "noble! He really does look noble!"

In the morning when they overslept —that is, when they didn't wake up as

124

early as the lynx waked up—the lynx would wait as long as he could make himself wait, and then would bound on the bed by the hunter, stand over him seriously, and very gently and carefully, his claws sheathed, try to open the hunter's eyes. So many mornings of his life the first thing the hunter knew was a big vague furry something pressing against his eyelids—and when at last, struggling up from sleep, he opened his eyes, the first thing he saw was the lynx's intent eyes staring into his.

"Having your eyes open really is the difference between being awake and asleep. It's very clever of him," the mermaid said.

"Very," the hunter agreed. "It's a queer way to wake up, though. The other morning I dreamed the moon was setting, and it kept getting bigger and redder and closer till I couldn't breathe, and I opened my eyes and there was the lynx."

The hunter and the lynx had a game that the hunter called boxing. The two of them sat three or four feet apart, poised, intent; then each would try to touch the other without the other's touching him. The hunter's hands and the lynx's forepaws shot out like a snake striking, as each of them hit, dodged, blocked, hesitated. The lynx was pretty good about keeping his claws in, but

126

occasionally he got too excited to remember, so that the hunter's shirts wore
out first up and down the sleeves.

"Velvet paws! velvet paws!" the
hunter would cry warningly.

The mermaid had got used to his saying it, but the first time she'd asked
perplexedly: "What's velvet?"

"I don't know," the hunter said.
"But it's what you say to a cat to get
him to keep his claws in. My mother
used to say it on the boat." So the
hunter said it and the mermaid and
the lynx understood it, each in his own
way—a little scrap of velvet there between the forest and the sea.

·VI·

THE LYNX
&
THE BEAR
BRING HOME
A BOY

Once for a day and two nights it stormed, stormed terribly; on the morning of the second day the clouds and the wind and the rain were gone, and the washed sky was full of sunlight. The lynx stood in the meadow and watched the hunter and the mermaid go away from him along the path that went up into the wood—the path was strewn with leaves and broken branches. Then he went down to the beach through the meadow, moving in great bounds; at the edge of the sand he stopped and shook from his fur, in a little shining cloud, the raindrops of the meadow-grass.

The beach's dark sand was all streaked and spotted with foam. He trotted along it, occasionally sniffing at the seaweed and driftwood—there were big soaked logs, even—that the storm had washed up to the edge of the grass. Farther along there was a dead seal, and the lynx went over to it and touched it with his paw.

When he came to the river, there was a lifeboat stranded at its edge: inside the boat something was crying.

The lynx went up, put his paws on the edge, and looked over. A woman was lying at the other end, half in and half out of the water that filled the bottom of the boat. She did not move, but the little boy who was huddled against her stopped crying, held out his hand to the lynx, and said hopefully: "Kitty! Kitty!"

The lynx trotted to the boy's end of the boat; the boy reached out to him and patted him on the head and the lynx purred. "Nice kitty! nice kitty!" said the boy. But in a minute the lynx drew away, his clear face clouding. Then all at once his eyes changed, and he started back up the beach.

When he got to the house he bounded in eagerly, but there was no one except the bear. The lynx went over and rubbed his head against him, but the bear didn't wake.

The lynx meowed, and tried to open the bear's eyes; and when that didn't work, he quite gently hit the bear on the nose. The bear's paws twitched. When the lynx hit him again, he put his paw over his head; at last he opened his eyes and staggered to his feet. The lynx ran to the door—but when the bear just stood there, the lynx came back, rubbed his head against him, and started off eagerly. This time the bear went too.

As they trotted along the beach the bear looked as dark and heavy and

134

hulking as the soaked logs they went by, but his eyes shone; the lynx's trips almost always ended in something good to eat. But this one ended in a stranded boat. The lynx put his paws on the edge and looked over; the bear stood on his hind legs and looked over.

The little boy was huddled against the woman, fast asleep. The lynx jumped into the boat, went up to the boy, and rubbed his face against the boy's face; in a while the boy's eyes opened and he reached out to the lynx. Then he saw the bear, on all fours now. He looked uneasy, and said to the lynx: "Kitty?" The bear walked to the boy's end of the boat and stuck his tremendous head over the edge. The boy drew back. But the bear looked too good-natured for the boy to keep on being afraid of him—in a minute he was petting the bear just as he had petted the lynx.

The lynx jumped down and started toward the house. Neither the boy nor the bear moved, so he came back to them. The boy put his arms around the bear's neck, laughing as he felt how thick and warm his fur was: when the bear started toward the lynx the boy lost his balance and fell out of the boat onto the sand. He wasn't hurt but, just the same, the lynx came over and rubbed his head against him. The boy

136

gave him two or three wavering pats, reached up and hugged the bear, and then burst into tears. He sat on the sand and cried—the lynx stood looking at him uneasily, and the bear sat there in the sunshine.

The boy stopped crying and hugged the bear again. Looking back over his shoulder, the lynx trotted off. The bear got up slowly and the boy, holding to the bear's fur, took two or three uncertain steps: then they started off. The boy looked very small and pale and the bear dark as a mountain, as they went slowly up the beach; the lynx, gray-silver and shining, flowed back and forth ahead of them like the tide. By the time they got to the meadow the boy was tired and lay down in the grass— the lynx ran ahead to the house, but it was empty. When he got back to the other two the boy was rested and went on.

When they came to the house the boy went in and looked expectantly around, but there was no one. The bear lay down by the fireplace, and the lynx rubbed against the boy and purred. But the boy was tired and hungry and fretful and didn't want to pet the lynx any more; he tried to climb up on the bed, but only pulled the bearskin down on top of himself. At last he went to where the bear was lying, curled up against him,

138

and fell asleep. Before long the bear was asleep too.

The lynx couldn't stay still; he would run out the door, trot up the path into the forest, start to turn back, go a few steps further, give a little mewing whine, and then pad back to the house. When at last he heard voices in the distance he bounded to the hunter and began to rub against his legs; as the hunter reached down and stroked his head he purred so loudly that the mermaid said, "He's acting the way he does when he brings us something he's caught."

The hunter said, "What have you got for us, boy? Got us another partridge?" The lynx ran ahead of them, ran back to them, ran ahead.

When the hunter and the mermaid came to the door and looked inside, their eyes blurred with sunlight, the room looked dark and empty except for the bear asleep by the fireplace. The lynx trotted over and stood proudly at his side, so that the mermaid said in perplexity, "He acts as if he'd brought us the bear."

The hunter walked over toward him —all at once he stopped and said unbelievingly: "Look!"

The mermaid came closer. Nestled against the bear's dark fur—his body had hidden it from her—there was

140

something fairer than the hunter, a little sleeping thing.

"A boy," the hunter said softly.

The lynx rubbed against his legs: he bent down and patted him, without taking his eyes off the boy. The mermaid reached out and touched the boy's white skin; then she said to the hunter, "He's so soft!" The hunter put his arm around her, and they stood there looking at the boy.

After a minute the mermaid said, "But how could he be here?" The hunter shook his head. "I don't know," he said. "I—I—"

He reached down and touched the boy the way you touch something in a dream, to make sure it is real. Suddenly his eyes widened and he said: "The storm, maybe. Maybe there're people on the beach. Maybe there're—"

He went over to the door and stared down at the sea; the mermaid sat passively by the boy. But in a minute he came back and said: "There's no one there."

The mermaid said: "I never knew what it was like when you lived here with your mother and father, I never had seen a little one. He's half like a little man and half—oh, *different!* His arms and legs are so short and white and his head's different—look how soft his hair and skin are! He looks all help-

142

less and not finished yet. He's so new!" ⁻

The hunter gave a queer sigh. He and the mermaid sat there looking at the boy. Somehow the hunter couldn't think of anything to say. He had a relaxed, satisfied look on his face; in a minute he actually yawned.

When the boy woke up they gave him little pieces of the lynx's last partridge and water out of a wooden cup. He reached out to the two of them as easily as he had reached out to the lynx, saying, "Mama! Mama!" to the mermaid; he laughed with pleasure when the hunter picked him up, but seemed not to know any name for him. The mermaid washed the boy and mar-

143

veled at his little shirt, so thin and dirty. "It's like your mother's handkerchief," she said to the hunter.

Later that day the hunter left for the beach. Before long he came back and got his shovel. "There's a boat washed up at the mouth of the river," he told the mermaid. "His mother's in it. She's dead."

The tracks of the lynx and the bear and the boy had shown him how the boy got to the house. He smoothed the boy's hair with his big hand and left; when he came home, hours after, his face looked absent and remembering, as if he were back with his own mother and father.

144

The lynx had stopped being proud of his find and had left for the forest. The bear lay by the fireplace and watched the mermaid playing with the boy; occasionally his paws would twitch, but he was a big bear now. The boy sat in the middle of the floor, and the mermaid would roll the leather ball to him, and he would pick it up and try to throw it back. But when he let go of it, it spun off any which way, and the mermaid had to scramble after it, unless it had rolled to where the hunter was. The hunter was playing with them, soon.

Whenever the boy picked up the ball or threw away the ball he would laugh a little high ringing laugh—a new sound in that big room, so used to the queer liquid laugh, the deep equable laugh, of the mermaid and the hunter. Sunset shone through the windows, and the room darkened; the hunter made a fire in the fireplace; and the boy held out his hands and warmed them at it.

"You can tell *he's* used to it," the mermaid said. "You can tell he's a—" She stopped and looked at the hunter, and said wistfully, "Remember when I wanted to pick up the coal?"

The hunter said to her, "I remember."

· VII ·

**THE
BOY**

In a little while they forgot that they had ever lived without the boy. Things would remind them, of course. "It feels strange to make them so small," the mermaid would say as she made the boy shoes and shirts and trousers of the softest, whitest deerskin, all covered with shell-patterns of birds and flowers. (She said about clothes, "I can see they're right for *him*.") And she made a deerskin cap, and then sewed so many bluejay feathers on it that you couldn't tell it was made of deerskin;

151

the boy's head was one blaze of blue.

The hunter made the boy four arrows and a bow as good as his own, only smaller. The boy wore them, but he was still too young to shoot with them, except when the hunter held his hands on the bow and bowstring. The hunter made him a little bed, covered it with the skin of a mountain lion, hung the bow and arrows over it, and every night put him in it together with his toys: the ball, and a fur bear, and a wooden lynx, and the hunter's necklace—so as not to hurt the mermaid's feelings, it was only lent to the boy—and the carvings of the hunter's father and mother. Sometimes the real lynx would come in the middle of the night, and in the morning when the boy awoke, the lynx would be there, curled at the bottom of the bed; the boy would reach down and stroke his head, and the lynx would yawn and give a sleepy purr. But the bear was too big for the bed; when he lay down by it his head went up past its head and his feet down past its foot.

The mermaid and the hunter and the boy went to the beach almost as much as the mermaid and the hunter had gone in the old days. The boy loved the sand and shells and little shallow waves that splashed in over his legs and stomach. Sometimes the hunter, with the boy in his arms, would wade out to where the

big waves were, and as some great green,
white-headed wave hung over them,
about to break, it would seem to the boy
that there was nothing in the world
strong enough to save them—then the
hunter would thrust himself up power-
fully, the wave would burst around
them in a smother of white, salt, blind-
ing foam, the boy would gasp and shut
his eyes, and when he opened them he
and the hunter stood there alone, the
wave was over.

In the little pool at the side of the
river, the mermaid taught the boy to
swim "the way I do, but with legs."
Before long swimming was as natural
to him as walking, just as hearing the

mermaid's stories, saying the mermaid's words were as natural to him as hearing the hunter's stories and saying the hunter's words. "He talks like one of the sea people," the mermaid said proudly. "Whatever he says has that watery sound."

The hunter gasped in his best Dolphin: "Help me! Help me to the beach!" and asked the mermaid whether it had a watery sound. The mermaid said, pointing: "You say it the way your father would. Whatever you say has that—that walnut sound."

"Let and live let," the hunter replied amicably. This was the way the mermaid had remembered "Live and let live," and the hunter hadn't corrected her, at first out of politeness and then because her way made better sense to him. Of course the mermaid had no idea that he was repeating her proverb, not his own.

Sometimes they would tell the boy how the lynx had come for them and led them to him, and how they had found him pressed up against the bear, fast asleep; once or twice they took him to the little marker the hunter had put over the mother's grave. But except for one or two confused, uneasy dreams, all the boy's memories were memories of the mermaid and the hunter; he *knew* that the hunter was his father and the

156

mermaid his mother and had always been. (The two of them were different from him, different from each other, but aren't a boy's father and mother always different from him, different from each other? The difference between the hunter and the mermaid was no greater, to the boy, than the difference between his father's short hair and trousers, his mother's long hair and skirts, is to any child.) The boy felt, "They're always telling me the lynx found me!" But he would smile at his father and mother and pretend the lynx had found him.

One day the hunter smiled back and said, "You must think you've lived with us always." The boy didn't know whether to say yes or no, and gave a laugh of confused joy, so that the mermaid smiled and said, "Yes, you think you've lived with us always."

The boy's heart beat faster, but he said, "No, the lynx found me." And this got to be a game of theirs. Because he knew it wasn't so, the boy enjoyed saying the lynx had found him; and the hunter and the mermaid enjoyed saying that the boy had lived with them always, because of—because of many things.

The boy went to sleep before the hunter and the mermaid and woke up before them; sometimes he and the lynx were the only things awake in the

158

house. The boy would sit up in his bed and look around at the hunter asleep under the bearskin, the mermaid asleep on top of it, the bear snoring by the fireplace, the hunter's bows and his own bow, the skins and shells and hunting horn, the blue-flowered, deer-hooved figurehead over the door, and there was not one thing there that, to the boy, was strange.

One night an hour or two after he'd gone to sleep, the sound of the rain waked him, and he heard his mother saying to his father: "He's so good and so clever, but he does grow slowly. I don't understand it. Remember how fast the bear grew? *And* the lynx."

159

The hunter didn't answer for a moment: he must have been remembering his own childhood. "I don't know," he said. "I don't think we grow as fast as they do. It seems to me I was a boy a long time—a long time."

The mermaid went on: "He's so different from our little ones. He's better than they are—they are bad little things —and he's a lot more interesting. He thinks of the queerest things."

"He does?"

"I should say so. He makes up undersea stories *he* tells *me*. This morning he told me that when he grows up he's going to make a bow and arrow you can shoot under water, and marry one of

160

the sea people and live with her at the bottom of the ocean."

"That's not so queer," the hunter retorted. "I've often thought of doing that myself."

The mermaid said blandly: "You think of the queerest things."

Next morning when the boy remembered hearing them, he didn't know whether or not it had been a dream. The part about growing slowly was important to him: he'd always lived with the mermaid and the hunter, he reasoned, and the bear and the lynx had come later and grown faster, that was why they were bigger. He liked having heard his father's "It seems to me I was a boy a

161

long time"—it seemed to him that he had been a boy a long time.

The days went by for him, all different and all the same. The boy was happy, and yet he didn't know that he was happy, exactly: he couldn't remember having been unhappy. If one day as he played at the edge of the forest some talking bird had flown down and asked him: "Do you like your life?" he would not have known what to say, but would have asked the bird: "Can you not like it?"

One bright blue morning the hunter and the mermaid started for the beach.

162

They left the boy in bed with his toys: he had a cold. The lynx was curled against him, looking lazy; the bear was asleep in the corner. "I'll carry you," said the hunter, and went down with the mermaid in his arms.

As she plunged in and out of the white surf the mermaid seemed something the sun had made from the light and shadows on the sea; her eyes dazzled you, like the little rainbows in the spray the waves flung up when they broke. She looked as much a part of the water as a fawn looks a part of the forest. She could, quite literally, swim circles around the hunter: he ploughed along with this sleek bubbling thing curving ahead and behind and on every side, occasionally shooting halfway out of the water like a dolphin. As they went home through the meadow, the hunter walking easily and the mermaid pushing herself along through the grass, the hunter said with a troubled smile: "To swim like that and then to live on land!"

"Oh well!" said the mermaid. She stopped and the hunter stopped—they sat there with the smell of the grass and flowers in their nostrils. The hunter yawned and stretched and with the backs of his hands rubbed the salt out of his eyes, and then leaned back and stared drowsily into the sky. The mermaid too looked off into nothing, and her face changed until at last she said: "The day I first went through your door I said to myself, 'Never since the world began has one of the sea people been here where I am.'"

She gave a queer laugh; then, still looking out unseeingly, she began to talk, and to talk, and to talk as she had never talked before.

"Remember when I wanted to pick up the coal?" she said. "Those days I— I'd picked it up, and it hadn't burnt me, and I sat there with it in my hands.

"In the morning when I'd wake I'd lie by you and say the new things to myself, and there were so many I couldn't believe I was awake, I'd say to myself: 'I'm dreaming.' And it was that way so long! But one morning when I started to think of the new things, there weren't any. And the next morning there still weren't any—and the next morning there still weren't. I was used to things.

"Only it was hard for me to get used to being alone so much. The sea people go in schools like fish, we're never alone. I'd wait for you and push myself across to the window, and think how long it would take me to push myself down over the meadow and the beach to the sea, and then I'd say to myself: 'Never since the world began has one

166

of the sea people been here where I am.'

"But that just meant that they'd been wrong and I was right, I'd tell myself. And I believed it. Only it was hard for me to believe it. And it was hard when I went back to them: they were so sorry for me, for the—"

Here the mermaid frowningly repeated some words, and went on: "That means, *the one who lives with the animals.* That's what they called me. The one who lives with the animals.

"The sea people don't know what a pet is—they couldn't understand why I wanted to live with animals, and land animals at that. And they don't know you or what you're like, to them you're a big animal from the land, and dangerous. When I went back to them they were always so sure that this time I would stay. And sometimes after I'd been with them a day or two, there where everything's so easy and the way it's always been, it was hard for me to believe that I was coming back to you. Sometimes it would seem to me that you and the house and the bed and the table were a dream I'd had and now I was awake—to get back to you I'd have to go to sleep again and dream the same dream.

"I remember I used to dream I lived on a ship and had legs, when I was little; and when I told my mother she

168

shook her head and said, 'Everything good comes from the sea.'

"But not for me! But not for me!" the mermaid said passionately. "Because the land *is* different. Sometimes the sea's rough, sometimes it's calm, but down underneath it's always the same. And life's like that, there. Once when I'd lived with you for years and years I'd gone back to them, and the second day was the same as the first, and the third day was the same as the second, and I began to feel so queer inside, I wanted something. It was like being hungry, only I wasn't hungry.

"And then I knew how you feel when it rains and there's nothing for you to do. I knew, but none of them knew. They don't know how to be bored or miserable. One day is one wave, and the next day the next, for the sea people —and whether they're glad or whether they're sorry, the sea washes it away. When my sister died, the next day I'd forgotten and was happy. But if you died, if he died, my heart would break.

"When it storms for the people, no matter how terribly it storms, the storm isn't real—swim down a few strokes and it's calm there, down there it's always calm. And death is no different, if it's someone else who dies. We say, 'Swim away from it'; we swim away from everything.

170

"But on land it's different. The storm's real, here, and the red leaves, and the branches when they're bare all winter. It all changes and never stops changing, and I'm here with nowhere to swim to, no way ever to leave it or forget it. No, the land's better! The land's better!"

The hunter stroked her shoulder and said in a serious thankful voice, "I'm glad it's better for you." He had learned something he had never known before: the mermaid could cry.

But the meadow was no different for the mermaid's tears or the hunter's knowledge; warm and soft and smelling of its flowers, it ran out green to the

171

sunny beach, green to the shadowy forest, and the hunter and the mermaid sat there in it. Below them the white-on-green of the waves was lined along the white shore—out beyond, the green sea got bluer and bluer till at last it came to the far-off blue of the island. There were small seals on the seal rocks, and the little gray spot out above the waves was a big black-and-white osprey waiting for a fish. But no fish came, and it hung there motionless. Everything lay underneath them like something made for them; things got smaller and smaller in the distance but managed, somehow, to fill the whole world.

"I'll carry you," said the hunter,

172

getting up; he went on with the mermaid in his arms. When he got to their door he put her down, they turned and looked at it all again, and then opened the door and went into the house.

"You were gone so *long!*" the boy said.

"Look at the shells I brought you," said the hunter, holding them out. The boy went through them carefully: there were two good enough to save. He put those with his own shells, and then went over them all one by one. Then he said to the mermaid: "The big one you brought me's still the best. The one from the bottom of the sea. These are good ones, but it's still the best."

"Yes, it's the reddest," the mermaid answered. "Down there it was all wet and purple, but up here it's"—she smiled at the hunter—"as red as red leaves. As red as a coal."

The boy asked, "Can't I get up now?"

"In a little," said the mermaid. "And because you were so good and stayed in bed all the time we were gone, I'll tell you a story."

The boy laughed with joy—there was nothing he liked better than the mermaid's stories. She sat down by him on the bed, and he moved over against her.

"Once upon a time," she began,

174

"long, long ago, there was a mermaid."

"Like you?"

"No, not like me, a little one—one so young and so small she could still swim through the little round windows in a ship. Remember the little round windows I showed you in the ship out past the seal rocks on the reef?"

"Where we got the lantern?"

"Where we got the lantern. Well, all one night, and the next day, and the next night, there was a great storm. The little mermaid and her people, instead of playing and fishing and looking for things by the rocks along the shore, swam a long way out to sea, where they could float far down under the waves—

175

it's always still, down there—or else
when they came to the top the waves
couldn't hurt them but would rock them
way up, and then *way* down, the way I
rock you: the way you'd rock if I put
you in the biggest branch of all, when a
tremendous wind is blowing, and the
branch goes way up in the air and then
bends so low it scrapes against the
ground.

"But finally the storm was over and
the sea people swam back to the shore.
The sea was all fresh and blue and
shining, and the sky was as blue as the
sea. When they got to the surf the
breakers crashed down around them
and flung the foam up over them, and

176

were as white as—as the snow when it's fallen in the night, and at morning you go to the window and look out and there still isn't a track on it: everything in the world is asleep except the snow."

The lynx waked up, yawned, and stretched, first with his front legs and then with his hind legs. Most of his winter fur was gone, so that his hind legs looked a size too large for his front legs, and his paws two sizes too large for any of the rest of him. He trotted to the door and meowed, and the hunter let him out.

The lynx started down through the meadow, and the hunter stood outside the door, half-listening to the story the mermaid was making up, and half-looking at—

He didn't know what he was looking at. He stretched with his front legs, like the lynx: that is, he held out his arms and tightened all the muscles and reached out as far as he could reach, for nothing. The lynx was already small in the distance; the bear came out of the door and sat down by the hunter.

The hunter heard the mermaid finish her story, and the boy thanked her for it. "That was a good one," he said warmly. "The sea ones are always the best. The sea's so—so—"

"You can get up now," the mermaid said. "Dress so you'll be good and

178

warm, and we can sit outside with your father."

When they came outside the boy was wearing the cap with the bluejay feathers, so that his head matched the sky. He went over and patted the bear and said to the hunter: "Where's the lynx?"

"Down there," answered the hunter, pointing; far along the beach, by the little river, you could see the tiniest lynx there ever was. The boy looked and saw him and said laughing, "That's where he found *me!*"

"Oh, we just told you that," said the hunter, starting their old game. "The very first day your mother and I came

179

to the house, there you were in the corner, fast asleep."

"That's right, fast asleep with *him*," said the boy, giving the bear a push.

"Oh no," said the mermaid, "that was years before the bear came. We've had you always."